HOLLER LOUDLY

CYNTHIA
LEITICH SMITH

·illustrated by·
BARRY GOTT

DUTTON CHILDREN'S BOOKS * An imprint of Penguin Group (USA) Inc.

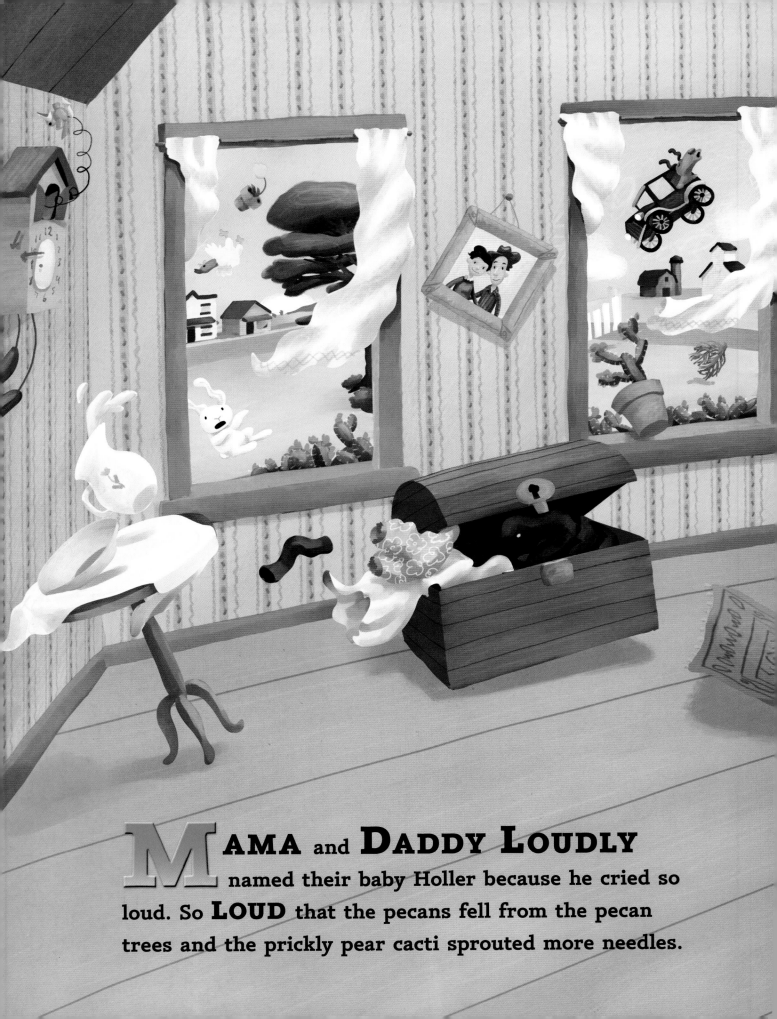

MAMA and **DADDY LOUDLY** named their baby Holler because he cried so loud. So **LOUD** that the pecans fell from the pecan trees and the prickly pear cacti sprouted more needles.

So **LOUD** that every hound dog in the county rolled up his ears and tossed back his head to bay. So **LOUD** the armadillos woke from their naps and the turkey vultures dropped their feathers.

"**HUSH!**" folks would tell Holler. "**HUSH!**"

Mama and Daddy loved their son. They tried everything to get Holler to speak more softly. When he was a baby, they said "hush" nicely.

When he was a toddler, they said "hush" sternly.

And finally, when he was old enough to go to school, they found themselves shouting **"HUSH!"** But it was no use.

Every few generations a Loudly baby was just born loud, and Holler had been a lucky one.

Holler loved school. He loved art and music. He loved reading and writing. And he loved facts and figures. But every time he exclaimed,

Yippee Ti Yi Yo! I Love Math!

his words came out too loud. So **LOUD** that Mr.
Smarty's chalk burst into dust and the students ducked
for cover.

Minnie Bell said, "Hush! Nobody cares!"

Jimmy Joe said, "Hush! You're annoying!"

And Mr. Smarty said, "Hush! No recess for you!"

Holler didn't like missing recess. How he wished
folks didn't mind his voice!

Holler loved to go to the big ole theater. He loved to stand in line for tickets. He loved to sit in the velvet seats. And he loved to see the show. But every time he exclaimed,

Yee Haw! I Love

Movies!

his words came out too loud. So **LOUD** that he rattled the chandelier and flattened Miz Poofy's hairdo.

The ticket seller called, "Hush! I'm trying to count change."

The lovebirds called, "Hush! Here come the previews."

And the usher called, "Hush! You've gotta go!"

Holler didn't like having to leave the movie theater. How he wished folks didn't mind his voice!

Holler loved fishing with Gramps and Gus. He loved baiting his hook with tamales. He loved floating in Gramps's boat. And he loved catching catfish. But every time he exclaimed,

Yahoo! Let's Land a BIG ONE!

his words came out too loud. So **LOUD** that the boat tipped, sending them soaring—*ker-splash!*—into the lake.

The catfish yelled, "Hush! We're outta here!"

Gus yowled, "Hush! There goes my dinner!"

And Gramps yelled, "Hush! No more fishing today!"

Holler didn't like being all wet. How he wished Gramps and cats and catfish didn't mind his voice!

Holler was feeling blue, so Mama and Daddy took him to the state fair. He loved cotton candy. He loved the Ferris wheel. And he loved the prizewinning livestock. But when he called,

SOO

Holler was so **LOUD** that the hogs broke free, then the cattle stampeded, and the whole fair shut down.

Mama's patience had run out. Daddy's devotion
had worn thin. But Gramps's barbershop quartet was
singing in town square. So they went to hear it.
Holler loved Gramps. He loved Gramps's cat Gus.
And he loved their barbershop quartet.

Howdy!

Concert

Looks Like Rain!

Holler yelled over the singing.

"Hush!" Daddy scolded.
"You're a distraction."

"Hush!" Mama scolded.
"Nobody can hear the music."

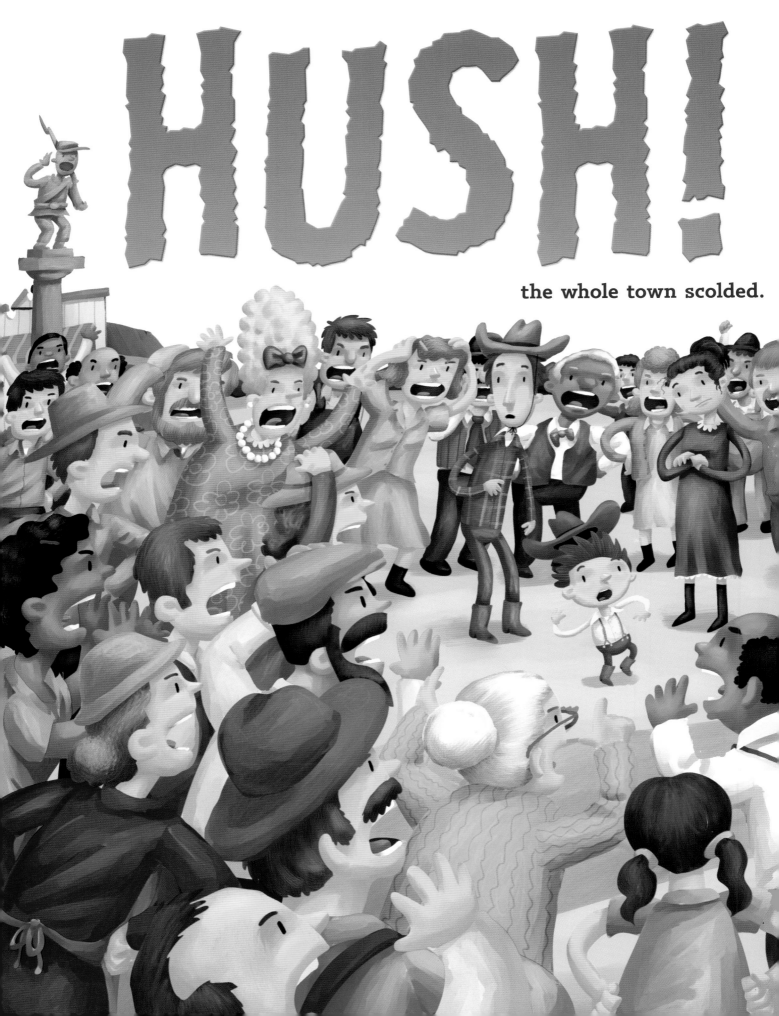

¡HUSH!

the whole town scolded.

So finally Holler hushed, and the quartet crooned
on. It didn't seem fair, though. Nobody was telling Mr.
Smarty to stop thinking or Miz Poofy to take down
her hair or Gus to give up fishing or Gramps to forget
his songs. Did folks want Holler to hush forever?
Being loud was part of who he was. Would they ever
appreciate his company, voice and all?

Holler took comfort, listening to the quartet. He loved songs about cowboys, and he loved songs about best girls. He loved songs about love and little dogies. And Holler realized something!

When he was quiet, he could listen better. Quiet times. . . could be just fine.

Just then, Holler looked to the sky. A tornado! It could flatten the town!

Right then, Holler knew in his heart that, sure, there were times to be quiet. But there were also times to be **LOUD!**

he bellowed, so **LOUD** that the land rolled and rumbled, rippled and shimmied and shook. So **LOUD** that ten-gallon hats soared into the sky. So **LOUD** that Mama and Daddy, Gramps and Gus, men and women, boys and girls sailed—*WhooooSH*—plum off their boot heels.

Go Away!

Holler shouted at the tornado,
which blew a raspberry at him.

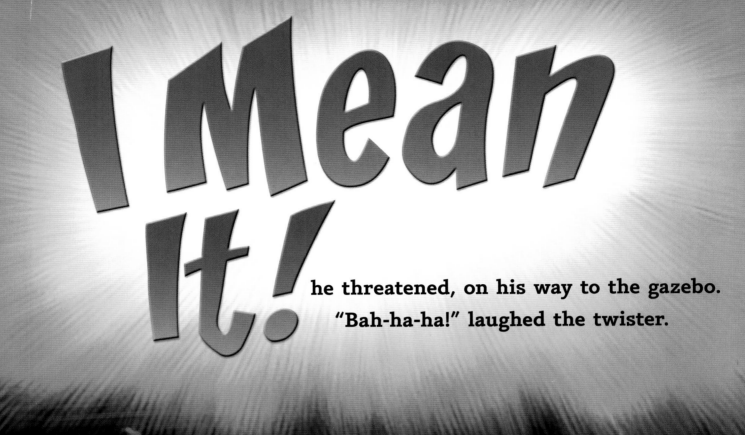

I Mean It!

he threatened, on his way to the gazebo.
"Bah-ha-ha!" laughed the twister.

Listen
Bag
This Here
And You'd
Skeda

Up You Big
of Wind!
Is My Town
Best
ddle!

And Holler was so **LOUD**, so **LOUD**, so absolutely, positively, knee-shakin', earth-quakin' **LOUD** that the tornado blew into a thousand sweet teeny breezy breezes—not one with an ounce of sass.

It was official! Not only was Holler the **LOUDEST** boy in history, he was also a hero! "Yippee ti yi yo!" everyone hollered. "Yee haw!"

"Yahoo, yahoo, yahoo, yahoo!" sang the barbershop quartet.

And Mama and Daddy sighed, "All righty."

"In the future," Gramps declared, "when you're loud, nobody's gonna mind."

So they all joined hands, cheered, and danced till the cows came home.

From that moment on, Holler was QUIET at QUIET times and **LOUD** at **LOUD** times.

The townsfolk were so delighted, they put his name on a very important sign.

To the Grandview (Missouri) branch of the Mid-Continent Public Library for first welcoming me as a young reader, back when libraries were almost always quiet. . . .

And to the Austin (Texas) Public Library for first welcoming me as a children's author, now that libraries are sometimes quiet and sometimes LOUD!

–C.L.S.

For Finn and Nandi

–B.G.

· ·

DUTTON CHILDREN'S BOOKS

A division of Penguin Young Readers Group

Published by the Penguin Group

Penguin Group (USA) Inc., 375 Hudson Street, New York, New York 10014, U.S.A. • Penguin Group (Canada), 90 Eglinton Avenue East, Suite 700, Toronto, Ontario M4P 2Y3, Canada (a division of Pearson Penguin Canada Inc.) • Penguin Books Ltd, 80 Strand, London WC2R 0RL, England • Penguin Ireland, 25 St Stephen's Green, Dublin 2, Ireland (a division of Penguin Books Ltd) • Penguin Group (Australia), 250 Camberwell Road, Camberwell, Victoria 3124, Australia (a division of Pearson Australia Group Pty Ltd) • Penguin Books India Pvt Ltd, 11 Community Centre, Panchsheel Park, New Delhi—110 017, India • Penguin Group (NZ), 67 Apollo Drive, North Shore 0632, New Zealand (a division of Pearson New Zealand Ltd) • Penguin Books (South Africa) (Pty) Ltd, 24 Sturdee Avenue, Rosebank, Johannesburg 2196, South Africa • Penguin Books Ltd, Registered Offices: 80 Strand, London WC2R 0RL, England

CIP Data is available.

Published in the United States by Dutton Children's Books, a division of Penguin Young Readers Group
345 Hudson Street, New York, New York 10014 • www.penguin.com/youngreaders

Designed by Jason Henry

Manufactured in China • First Edition
ISBN: 978-0-525-42256-3

1 3 5 7 9 10 2 6 4 2